Namm, Diane.
Rikki-Tikki-Tavi moves in

22.00 01/08

THE JUNGLE BOOK

by Rudyard Kipling

#1 Rikki-Tikki-Tavi
Moves In

Adapted by Diane Namm
Illustrated by Jim Madsen

Spotlight

Sterling Publishing Co., Inc.
New York

visit us at www.abdopublishing.com

Reinforced library bound edition published in 2008 by Spotlight, a division of the ABDO Publishing Group, 8000 West 78th Street, Edina, Minnesota 55439. Published by agreement with Sterling Publishing Co., Inc.

Originally published and © 2006 by Barnes and Noble, Inc.
Illustrations © 2006 by Jim Madsen
Cover illustration by Jim Madsen

Library of Congress Cataloging-in-Publication Data
This title was previously cataloged with the following information:
Namm, Diane.
    The jungle book. #1, Rikki Tikki Tavi moves in / by Rudyard Kipling ; adapted by Diane Namm ; illustrated by Jim Madsen.
        p. cm. -- (Easy reader classics)
    Summary: A brief, simplified retelling of the episode in "The Jungle Book" during which a very curious mongoose becomes a house pet and races a snake to see who will be "Master of the Garden."
    [1. Mongooses--Fiction. 2. Cobras--Fiction. 3. India--Fiction.] I. Kipling, Rudyard, 1865-1936.
II. Madsen, Jim, 1964- ill. III. Title: Rikki-tikki-tavi. IV. Title.
PZ7.N14265 Jun 2006
[E]--dc22   2005031306
ISBN 978-1-59961-336-9 (reinforced library bound edition)

Contents

The Big Flood

One morning,
a very curious little
mongoose said,
"Today I want
to explore.
I want to explore
my burrow!"
So he started to dig.

This little mongoose
was a little *too* curious.
He did not listen
when raindrops started
falling from the sky.
He only dug deeper.
He just *had* to know
how far down he could go!

He did not see
the lightning.
He did not hear
the thunder.

He did not see or hear

anything at all until . . .

Whish! Whoosh!
Water poured
into the burrow.

It carried him into the garden—
the garden in front of the house
the little boy
lived in.

Mongoose Trouble

"May we keep him, Mama?"
asked the little boy.
"Teddy," Mama said to him,
"you know a mongoose
can cause a lot of trouble."
"Not this one!" said Teddy.
"Not my mongoose,
Rikki-tikki-tavi!"
Teddy carried Rikki
into the house.

Rikki-tikki-tavi had never been
inside a house before.
He was very curious—
a little *too* curious!

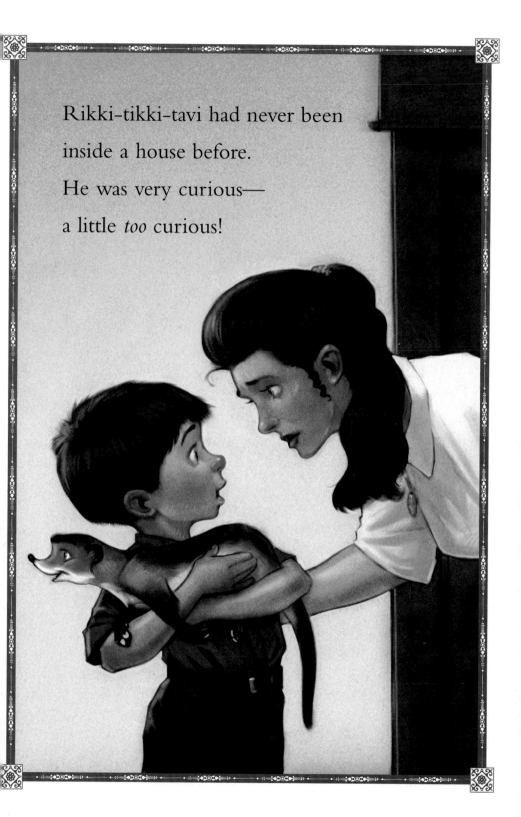

He just *had* to know
what was in those sacks.
He just *had* to know
what was under
that plant.

The little boy
chased Rikki around.
Mama's lamps and vases
crashed to the floor.

"Teddy," said Mama,

"that mongoose must go!"

"Please, Mama," Teddy said.

"Give him one more chance."

"Well, all right," said Mama.
"He can stay—for now—
but not in my house.
Go run and play outside."

In the Garden

Rikki and Teddy played
all morning long.
Rikki showed Teddy
how to play
the mongoose way.
They explored the garden.
They dug a big hole
deep in the ground.

"It's time for lunch!"
Mama called.
Teddy told Rikki
to wait for him
in the garden.
"Do not go into
the tall, tall grass,"
said Teddy.

Rikki was very curious.
What could be in
the tall, tall grass?
He just *had* to know!
He tiptoed into it.
Suddenly . . .

... out popped a snake!

"Who are *you?*" Snake hissed.

"Who are *you?*" asked Rikki.

"I am Snake," Snake hissed.

"Snake, Master of the Garden."

"No you are not!"

said Rikki.

"Snake, you are not

Master of the Garden!

The garden belongs to me—

to Teddy and me!"

Just then,
Teddy came out
of the house.
"Rikki-tikki-tavi!
Let's play!" Teddy called.

"I have to go," Rikki said.

"Wait," hissed Snake.

"I have an idea."

Rikki knew he should
go to Teddy—
but he was too curious.
He just *had* to know
Snake's idea!

The Race

"You think *you* are
Master of the Garden,"
hissed Snake,
"and I think I am.
So, little mongoose,
why don't we race?
Whoever wins will be
the one and only
Master of the Garden."

"A race from where
to where?" Rikki asked.
"From here to there,"
hissed Snake.
Then he took off—
straight for Teddy.

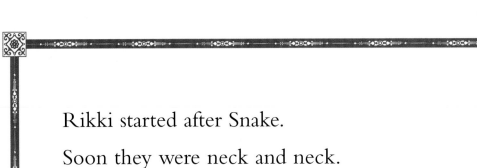

Rikki started after Snake.

Soon they were neck and neck.

Then Rikki passed Snake!

Rikki was so excited,

he forgot to look where he was going.

He forgot the hole

he and Teddy dug that morning . . .

and down he went!

"Ouch," he said. "My paw!"

Rikki quickly got up.

He peeked his head

out of the hole.

Oh, no! he thought.

Snake is winning!

Rikki knew he did not
have much time.
He jumped out of the hole.
He jumped as high as he could.
He jumped over Snake—

and into Teddy's arms!

Just then, Teddy saw Snake.

"Oh, a snake," said Teddy.

"Snakes are dangerous.

Into the house, Rikki!"

Teddy saw that Rikki

had hurt his paw.

He ran into the house.

"Mama," he said, "Rikki is hurt!"

"Oh, poor little mongoose,"
Mama said, bandaging his paw.
"You are just a little
too curious, aren't you?"

"Rikki needs us, Mama,"
Teddy said. "Can't he stay?"
Mama looked down at Rikki.
He snuggled deeper in her arms.
"All right, Teddy," said Mama,
"but I hope he can learn
to be a little less curious!"
Don't worry, Mama,
Rikki thought.
I might never
be curious enough
to leave this safe home!